**For Growth Hungry** Business Owners

# GET10X
# DONE

Drive 10 Times
More Results
In Your Business
& Personal Life.

**For Growth Hungry** Business Owners

# GET10X DONE

Drive 10 Times
More Results
In Your Business
& Personal Life.

## RAJIV PASRICHA

Worldwide Published by
Pendown Press

**PENDOWN PRESS**

**An ISO 9001 & ISO 14001 Certified Co.,**

**Regd. Office:** 2525/193, 1st Floor, Onkar Nagar-A, Tri Nagar, Delhi-110035

**Ph.:** 09350849407, 09312235086

**E-mail:** info@pendownpress.com

**Branch Office:** 1A/2A, 20, Hari Sadan, Ansari Road, Daryaganj, New Delhi-110002

**Ph.:** 011-45794768

**Website:** PendownPress.com

**First Edition:** 2023

**ISBN:** 978-93-5554-545-9



*Layout and Cover Designed by* Pendown Graphics Team

*Printed and Bound in India by* Thomson Press India Ltd.

# Contents

# About The Author

Rajiv Pasricha is a renowned Business Growth Consultant, a highly-respected Transformative Facilitator, and a seasoned entrepreneur with 30+ years of rich experience.

Alumni of the prestigious SRCC, New Delhi, he holds coaching, facilitating and hiring certifications from Franklin Covey India, Leadership Management International Inc., USA and Performia International, Sweden, respectively.

Over the course of his personal and professional life, Rajiv has faced and successfully overcome numerous obstacles that came in the way of achieving his goals. From battling nagging weight loss issues to working hard but failing to achieve an exponential and consistent growth in his business, Rajiv has seen it all...

However, the two things that have helped him come out of stagnation and move towards excellence are his never-say-die spirit and an unwavering quest to find a tried-and-tested framework to overcome every obstacle holding him back from achieving his true potential.

He has personally coached  more than 600 business owners and trained more than 70,000 people over the years.

*Deep gratitude to Akshar Yadav,
Neeru Gupta, Daljit Singh,
Shailendra Vijayvergia, and Rohit Kumar.
Your efforts have given
this work its heart and soul.
I can't thank you enough.*

# Acknowledgements

Echoing the timeless wisdom that 'it takes a village to raise a child', this book has been sculpted by a chorus of diverse influences. Direct contributions and subtle inspirations, each person acknowledged, have etched a unique mark on its pages.

**To my beloved parents** - Although you are not with me physically, your enduring love, blessings, and warmth permeate every moment of my life and inspire me to attain greater heights.

**To my dear sons**- Raunaq and Joy, your genuine interest and whole-hearted involvement in my work, paired with your thoughtful suggestions, have accelerated my progress and filled my journey with warmth and joy. Your support is my greatest motivation.

**To my extended family**- Vashnoo Malhotra, Anjula Malhotra, Anil Sarin, Lakshmi Sarin, Mukesh Thukral, Priyanka, Afzal, Divya, Janesh, Simran, Jasmine, Gautam & Raghav - I want to express my deepest gratitude for your unwavering support, limitless affection, and constant motivation that have served as the foundation of my personal journey. I am eternally grateful for your presence and blessings in my life.

**I am deeply grateful to L. Ron Hubbard, Mr Horst, Tapan Gayary and all the staff at the Religious Foundation of Scientology of New Delhi**- Your wisdom, constant support, and genuine intentions have made the most profound impact on my life.

**I sincerely thank my mentors and coaches**- Shyam sir, Pradeep Bhatt, Sama Taneja, Neeru Gupta, Rekha Nag, Bharti Gupta, Varinder Kumar, Bernard Percy, Deepak Soni & Amit Chawla. Your invaluable support and guidance have been instrumental in shaping my journey, and without you, I would not have reached the position I currently occupy.

**Honouring my late grandparents, sister, uncles, aunties, and cousins**- Sardari Lal Pasricha, Kartar Devi Pasricha, Ramnath Kalra, Tarawanti Kalra, Manjula Thukral, Somnath Kalra, Shakuntla Kalra, Dinanath Kalra, Suhagwanti Kalra, Bal Kishan Pasricha, Jaswant Rani, Iqbal Narayan Pasricha, Santosh Pasricha, Janakdulari Sachdev, Jagdish Singh Sachdev, Ajit Singh Sachdev, Om Prakash Kalra, Shashi Kalra, Renu Kalra, S P Kalra, Kusum Kalra, Subhash Kalra, Rajinder Arora, Sunil Kalra, Ruby Kalra, Shafique Ahmed, Nazifa Ahmed, Krishan Kumar Sehgal, Ashok Malhotra, Mulak Raj Malik, Mohini Malik, Yogender Mohan Pasricha– I will forever hold the joy and love you brought into my life.

**To my Paternal and Maternal Relatives**- Kailash Kalra, Geeta Kalra, Poonam Kalra, Indu Kalra, Ramesh Kalra, Kiran Kalra, Avinash Kalra, Rajni Kalra & Saroj Arora - the warmth of your blessings and love are a heartfelt treasure. I am deeply grateful for your constant support and encouragement.

*Acknowledgements*

**To my dear Uncles and Aunties-** Raksha Khurana, Surinder Kaur Chawla, Aroon Kumar, Neelu Yadav, Veena Bawa, Anju Malhotra, Dharmesh Jaitly, Saroj Jaitly, Hira Lal Jain, Satya Jain, Sudesh Sehgal, Subhash Bhatia, Kamla Bhatia, Parveen Thapar, Sushil Bhatia & Sarla Bhatia- your continuous blessings and love have been an immense source of comfort in my life. I am deeply grateful for your affection and support.

**To my closest friends-** Gautam, Stephie, Bhawna, Nassif, Sharan, Bhavna, Akshar, Payal, Satinder, Nisha, Manish Seth, Sonal, Gaurav, Aarti, Ajay, Anju, Vineet Kapur, Parag, Neenu, Vineet Bhatia, Anshu, Smita, Ravi, Saru, Ashutosh, Vinod, Manish Kohli, Shalika, Nafis Khan & Amaan-ul-Haq- Your unwavering companionship, filled with warmth and sincerity, has profoundly enriched my life in countless ways. Your presence is a cherished gift I hold very close to my heart.

**I extend my deepest gratitude to the remarkable 'Unstoppables' Group.** Your combined resilience and support have been instrumental in helping me overcome hurdles and achieve the ambitious task of writing this book within the designated time frame. The magnitude of your contribution to this endeavour is beyond measure and deeply valued.

**To my coachees-** Gaurav Bawa, Meenu Bawa, Aakash Goyal, Tina Goyal, Puneet Agarwal, Swati Agarwal, Aryan Agarwal, Aditi Bansal, Kshitij Bansal, Alok Agarwal, Vandana Agarwal, Amit Sehgal, Ritu Sehgal, Amit Mittal, Swati Mittal, Rajnish Patwari, Asha Patwari, Shefali Tripathi, Daljit Singh, Harsh Gupta, Gunpreet Kaur, Gaurav Soni, Narjeet Soni, Puneesh Singla, Rachna Singla, Sudhir Agarwal, Rishi Verma,

Mohan Gupta, Pooja Bansal, Gurmukh Singh, Vipul Maheshwari, Archana Maheshwari, Prashant Mittal, Sanjay Singhania, Nikhil Bothra, Manish Gulati, Jyoti Gulati, Rajat Gupta, Amit Arora, Vijay Wadhawan, Pawan Wadhawan, Jai Bhagwan Goyal, B S Chadha, Manjeet Singh Chadha, Amardeep Singh Chadha, Jagdeep Singh Chadha, Ajit Pal Sethi, Ravi Shankar, Ravinder Agarwal, Saurabh Agarwal, Rajesh Vig, Ritu Vig & Abhishek Vig - our relationship has evolved beyond the professional realm into a heartfelt connection that is truly special. I am deeply grateful for the respect, warmth, and encouragement you continually provide.

**To my cherished cousins & their spouses** - Vinod Pasricha, Usha Pasricha, Sharda Pasricha, Neelam Pasricha, Sweety Sachdev, Kapil Pasricha, Sushma Pasricha, Deepak Malik, Ruby Malik, Manoj Malik, Pummy Malik, Anil Kalra, Ruchi Kalra, Sunny Kalra, Jyotsna Kalra, Seema Kwatra, Deepak Kwatra, Suparna Sethi, Rajeev Sethi, Rajiv Kalra, Tanu Kalra, Tinka Batra, Mahesh Batra, Varun Kalra, Prashant Kalra, Aman Kalra, Dipankar, Shivangi, Kaajal, Dipti, Tanu, Surbhi, Sarita Sahu, Nikka & Vinni - your enduring love, encouragement, and the precious moments we have shared are forever etched in my heart. I am deeply grateful for your support in my life.

**To my neighbours-** Gita ji, Saikat, Lopa, Avery, and Ira - your warm and friendly presence has created a nurturing environment, and your unwavering cheerfulness and constant encouragement have been an uplifting source of support. I am grateful for the positive energy you infuse to our community.

**To my dear childhood friends & their spouses-** Tarun Sehgal, Sangeeta Mehra, Vijay Malhotra, Babita Malhotra, Preeti Wadhera, Sidharth Wadhera, Rajiv Jaitly, Sarika Jaitly, Alok Jain, Amit Jain, Satyendra Shukla & Seema Shukla-although our paths have diverged and our meetings have become infrequent over the years, the subtle warmth and encouragement from our shared past continue to resonate in my life. Even though your presence may be distant, it is cherished and provides enduring support.

**Deep appreciation for my teachers and friends at Frank Anthony Public School.** Your guidance, support, and the school's motto, "Courage is destiny," have been vital in shaping my path.

**To the esteemed members of the Community of Scientologists of Delhi-** I want to express my admiration and appreciation for each and every one of you: Arjun Anand, Geeta Anand, Seema Baweja, Vasu, Astha Singh, Puneet Bhogra, Arti Bhogra, Manju, Subhash Palsule, Sujata Palsule, Amit Chopra, Priyanka Chopra, Abhishek Juneja, Dushyant Kamra, Jolly Kamra, Satinder Singh, Devender Agarwal, Ravinder Kumar, Ruby Khanduja, Sukhvinder Singh, Prashant Verma, Ravinder Kumar, Neeraj Agarwal, Sumit Bhatt, Pradeep Kathuria, Harwinder Kamra, Ravinder Sain, Rohit Agarwal, Pooja Agarwal, Vikas Gupta, Rekha Nag, Karan Kochar, Monica Kochar, Sanjay Sharma, Madhuri Sharma, Amit Sethi, Tanya Sethi, Arneet Kaur, Madhu Jhunjhunwala, Shikha, Somya Budhia, Ananya Budhia, Sanjeev Gupta, Sunita Gupta, Deepti Vijayvergia, Rohit Sharma, Mukta Bhatt, Arohi Bhatt,

Rajeev Ghose, Anjali Thakur, Vijaya Talwar, Kiara Bhogra, Geet Vijayvergia, Siya Vijayvergia, Abhidev Palsule, Sumukh Kumar, Urvi Bajaj, Luna Bajaj, Veer Bhogra, Lakshay Kochar- your dedication to inspiring one another, nurturing continuous spiritual growth, and striving to create a positive change in the society is truly commendable. I am grateful to be a part of such a devoted and uplifting ecosystem.

**Big thanks to Dinesh Verma and his remarkable team-** They kept the dream of this book alive and helped it become a reality.

**To Vicky, my hairdresser for the last 20 years, Vikrant, my fitness coach and Ashok Gupta, my masseur-** your exceptional service and genuine care play a significant role in helping me maintain my health and professional appearance. I am deeply grateful for your dedication & support.

**To the exceptional team at Get 10X Done Academy-** Rohit, Parvati, Jitender, Sanjay and Akhilesh - your professionalism and dedication ensure a seamless operation, allowing me to trust that our customers will consistently enjoy a world-class experience. I am deeply grateful for your unwavering commitment and hard work.

**Lastly, I want to acknowledge myself-** for my relentless quest to understand human complexities and dedication to my purpose.

# Testimonials

"Before I enrolled in Rajiv's Coaching Program, my life was a battlefield filled with stress, anger, and confusion. But his program was the peace treaty I needed. This program was the turning point in my life. It has helped me increase my profits by 100% while teaching me the importance of communication, happiness, and purpose. Now, I lead with confidence and clarity, and my relationships have never been better."

**~Gaurav Bawa**
*CEO, Bawa Jewellers Pvt. Ltd.*
*www.bawajewels.com*

"Navigating life was like walking in a dark tunnel before encountering Rajiv's Coaching Program. It was an eye-opener that illuminated my path, helping me transform my stress and anger into calmness and focus. I've seen a 40% rise in my sales, but more importantly, I've become a happier, healthier individual with solid relationships and clear life goals. I can't thank Rajiv enough for this tremendous transformation!"

**~Daljit Singh**
*Director: Excellence and Innovation, Newage Concepts India (P) Ltd*
*www.newage-concepts.com*

"The 10X Coaching Program helped me identify roadblocks in my personal and professional life and gave me the tools to eliminate them. I doubled my turnover in 6 months with jet speed. My happiness quotient has increased significantly. Thank You, RP!"

**~Shefali Tripathi**
*(International Recruitment Strategist)*
*Director, Career Genii Pvt Ltd.*
*www.careergenii.in*

"Rajiv has been invaluable in helping me navigate professional and personal challenges, most notably a dispute with my brother and business partner. His unique wisdom tool and communication framework have elevated our team's productivity and improved my family relationships, leading to an increased sense of fulfilment and inner peace. Remarkably, we made substantial progress towards all our initial intentions by the end of our work together. I can't recommend Rajiv enough if you're determined to enhance your leadership skills and seek genuine happiness. His guidance has indeed been a game-changer!"

**~Narjeet Soni**
*Co-Founder & Innovation Strategist, Lean Apps GmbH*
*www.theleanapps.com*

"Rajiv sir's Coaching has been a game-changer for me. It has empowered me to take charge, streamline processes, and forge genuine connections with my team, leading to outstanding team performance. The program has also given me the remarkable ability to balance work and family life, fulfilling me more. I can't thank Rajiv sir enough for his guidance in my journey towards becoming an exceptional leader!"

**~Pawan Wadhawan**
*Director, Sipcon Technologies Pvt Ltd.*
*www.sipconinstrument.com*

"Before joining The 10X Coaching Program, I was a boat adrift in the ocean, battered by the waves of stress and confusion. His program became my compass, guiding me towards clarity in my goals and helping me listen and connect with those around me. My profits soared by 30%, and I found a new found appreciation for my health and well-being. I've become not just a better leader but a better person. Thank you, Rajiv sir!"

**~Rajnish Patwari**
*Director, KK House Hold Pvt. Ltd.*
*www.steelobrite.com*

"Before collaborating with Rajiv, I felt lack of power in my personal and professional life, lacking deep relationships and struggling with productivity and time management. However, Rajiv's mentorship has been transformative. Through our coaching sessions, he helped me foster self-confidence and awaken my inner leader, providing me with practical skills and strategies that have significantly improved all areas of my life. Empowered by Rajiv's guidance, I now feel equipped to take control of my life and shape my desired future. For anyone seeking personal and business growth, I wholeheartedly recommend Rajiv."

**~Gaurav Soni**
*Co-Founder &, Product Strategist, Lean Apps GmbH*
*www.theleanapps.com*

"Thank you, Rajiv, for this incredible journey! I was consumed by fear and confusion, unable to establish good relationships or set clear goals. This program has been a sanctuary, teaching me the art of effective communication and the essence of happiness. My profits surged by 42%, but more than that, I have found a new zeal for life!"

**~Puneesh Singla**
*Co-Founder & CTO, Lean Apps GmbH*
*www.theleanapps.com*

# Introduction

Imagine a life where you consistently accomplish ten times more than you ever thought possible. A life where you tap into your hidden potential, attain greatness, and create a life that is not only successful but profoundly fulfilling and meaningful. This is the promise of "Get 10X Done," a book that will unlock the missing elements essential for your extraordinary success.

As a leadership coach and avid learner, I have interacted with numerous coaches, mentors, and guides who shared their wisdom and insights. These invaluable gems of wisdom, gathered over my journey, have explosively transformed my life and those with whom I have worked. I have curated only four of these gems to share with you in this book.

"Get 10X Done" is not just another self-help book. It is a compilation of 4 guiding principles that will lead you towards achieving remarkable results as a business owner or anyone who is seeking to accelerate their progress. If you have taken countless self-improvement initiatives, immersed yourself in learning, and still not moving ahead with the desired pace, then this book is for you.

One of the major breakthroughs you will experience is a heightened awareness of real connections. You will see the interplay between different aspects of your life and understand how they influence each other. Moreover, you will unlock the power of contribution and recognize the unbelievable impact you can make on the world around you.

As you dive into the pages of this book, you will embark on a transformative journey comprising 4 chapters: Unleashing the Power of Duty: Your Path to Peak Motivation, Design a Beautiful Life: Tap into the Power of Vision, Threads of Grace: Exploring the Dynamic Duo of Help and Gratitude and Building High Trust Relationships: A Path to Joy and Fulfillment. By embracing these concepts, you will get the invaluable tools and insights to drive yourself toward 10X success.

"Get 10X Done" is not a mere collection of theoretical concepts. It is a practical guide with thought-provoking content to help you develop new understandings and be able to implement them in your life. This book will feel like a meaningful conversation, building a sense of connection and camaraderie as we travel this transformative journey together.

Are you ready to step into your greatness? Are you prepared to embrace the missing elements that will help unlock your hidden potential? If so, let's embark on this remarkable adventure together and create a unique, beautiful and extraordinary life.

# Chapter 1

# Unleashing the Power of Duty: Your Path to Peak Motivation

Welcome, my friend, to the incredible journey of unleashing the power of duty within you. In this chapter, we will explore how embracing duty as a motivator can drive you towards peak motivation and enable you to accomplish what may seem impossible. So, please grab a cup of your favourite beverage, settle in, and dive into this transformative concept together.

## The Essence of Duty: "If not me, then who?"

Imagine a mother diligently nurturing her child, sacrificing her comfort and sleep to ensure her child's well-being. Consider a soldier standing tall on the frontlines, driven by a profound sense of duty to safeguard his fellow soldiers and protect his nation. Envision a great king shouldering the responsibility of his kingdom, making difficult decisions with the welfare of his people at heart. What is the similarity among these individuals? They operate from a deep-rooted sense of duty, a driving force that compels them to act and achieve greatness.

## Understanding Duty

Duty, my friend, is far more than a mere obligation to achieve external rewards or meet societal expectations. It is an internal compass that guides us to take responsibility for our lives and the lives of those around us. Duty demands that we question ourselves, "If not me, then who?" It calls us to step up, rise above mediocrity, and tap into our brilliance.

## The Power of Duty

When duty becomes our motivator, something extraordinary happens. We tap into the natural wellspring of determination, resilience, and perseverance. Duty fuels our actions and propels us forward, even in adversity. It ignites a fire within us that refuses to be extinguished. When duty becomes our driving force, we become unstoppable.

## A Powerful Testament to Duty: From a Naive Boy to a Successful Businessman

Please allow me to share a powerful testament to duty, a personal narrative that illustrates its transformative power.

In August 1987, a chilling encounter disturbed our tranquil life. Three men, who appeared like gangsters, pounded on our door, demanding money that my parents owed from their failing business. We were in a big financial mess. As the youngest child, a 19-year-old college student in a family with three sisters, two of whom were married, I felt a shiver of fear and anxiety.

At that crossroads, I found myself confronted with two choices: to step back, clinging to my youthful innocence, or to step forward, embracing the responsibilities of adulthood. I could have hidden behind my age, just a young man on his college journey at Sriram College of Commerce. But when I looked into the worried eyes of my parents, my father, who had reluctantly transitioned from a government servant to a businessman, and my mother, who supported him, a voice inside me said, **"If not me, then who?"**

Determined, I chose the latter path. I immersed myself in the vortex of our business, juggling between my academic pursuits and the complex business predicaments. Despite overwhelming obstacles, I persevered, driven by my newfound sense of duty and resilience.

After a challenging 2.5 years, I had not only graduated with a degree in  Economics but also succeeded in reversing our business's fortunes, transforming it into a profitable entity. Throughout this journey, I underwent my own transformation, evolving from a naive boy into a responsible and determined young man. The sight of pride and relief in my parents' eyes remains my most cherished reward, a testament to the choice I made in the hour of need.

## Embracing Duty in the 4 Key Roles of Your Life

Now, let's explore how the sense of duty can manifest in different life roles.

Consider your role as a business owner. What is your duty? It is to build an ever-expanding organization, with sufficient cash reserves, delivering world-class goods & services and the staff members are highly productive and very well remunerated.

Your duty is to create a positive impact in the lives of your employees, customers, and the community. It goes beyond the pursuit of profit. It is to lead with integrity, foster a challenging & nurturing work environment, and inspire others to attain greatness.

As a parent, your duty is to foster children who are competent, self-assured, accountable, ethically aware, and filled with joy.

It extends beyond fulfilling your children's basic needs. It is your duty to guide, nurture, and instill values that will shape their character and enable them to thrive. You are their role model, source of inspiration and support. Embrace this duty with love and dedication.

As a spouse, your duty is to contribute in creating a beautiful relationship where your partner feels deeply loved, respected & cared for.

Duty encompasses more than shared responsibilities. It is a commitment to prioritize communication and strive to bring out the best in each other.

As a caretaker of yourself, your duty is to first preserve your health (above all other responsibilities) and relentlessly pursue mental and spiritual advancement.

Self-care, personal growth, and well-being are not luxuries but responsibilities we owe ourselves. Amidst our obligations to others, we often neglect an essential duty: the duty towards ourselves. By nurturing ourselves, we become better equipped to fulfil our responsibilities towards others. Make self-care a priority and honour the commitment you have towards yourself.

As we conclude this chapter, let the essence of duty resonate within you. Just like a mother, soldier, or great king achieves the seemingly impossible through their unwavering dedication to duty, acknowledge the multiple roles you play in life and embrace your responsibilities wholeheartedly.

Let the new understanding of duty guide your actions, motivate, and fuel your journey toward personal and professional fulfilment. Remember, duty is not a burden but a privilege. It empowers you to make a substantial impact and create an enduring legacy.

# Chapter 2

# Design a Beautiful Life: Tap into the Power of Vision

Now, let's look at something interesting. When we build our homes, plan weddings, or go on vacations, we plan and consider each and every little detail. It's like a well-choreographed dance. But here's the mind-boggling part: Do we put the same effort into designing our lives?

Are we living by design or just going along for the ride? It's time to ponder.

Imagine life as a blank canvas. We are the artists endowed with the power to transform this canvas into a remarkable piece of art. However, to breathe life into this canvas, we need a deep understanding of our unique colours - our strengths, the unexplored potential we possess and our deepest desires. This understanding is a vital element to create a beautiful life.

How do we add those vibrant strokes to the canvas of our life?

We will tackle the "how" in 2 simple steps.

The first step is to understand yourself deeply.

The great Greek philosopher Socrates said, "Know thyself." It sounds simple, but it's a potent phrase. Understanding your deepest desires, strengths & weaknesses, forms the foundation of a meaningful life.

At this point, I want to share a thought-provoking fable that explains the importance of recognizing our strengths and weaknesses.

Imagine a world where animals have a school to help their young ones tackle the problems of the new age. They, too, with the best intentions, decide that all their children should learn everything — running, climbing, swimming, and flying. But as we will see, this approach leads to a paradoxical situation.

The duck, a natural swimmer, is made to focus on running, leading to wear and tear of his webbed feet. This eventually results in his swimming skills becoming just average.

The rabbit, meanwhile, becomes an object of ridicule, her fur matting and making it look like a rat during swimming classes, causing it immense distress.

Interestingly, the eagle, who effortlessly outperforms everyone in climbing, uses his unique method to reach the top. However, his individualistic approach is considered unacceptable, leading to harsh disciplinary actions.

The fish, born without legs and unable to breathe out of the water, is forced into running and climbing classes, causing it to despise school.

This situation reaches a point where the fish, who excels in swimming, is relieved from the swimming classes to receive private tutoring in running and climbing.

The concluding scene of the fish seeking political asylum in Canada starkly reflects the frustration and misery caused by not acknowledging her innate strengths.

This fable highlights a critical life lesson:

**Let the fishes swim.**

**Let the rabbits run.**

**Let the eagles fly.**

**The question is, should you swim, run or fly?**

The fact is, **"You cannot be anything you want to be, but you can become more of who you truly are"**.

Peter Drucker says:

**"Most People think they know what they are good at. They are usually wrong. And yet, a person can perform only from strength."**

**"To succeed in this new world, we will have to learn, first, who we are. Few people, even highly successful people, can answer the question: Do you know what you're good at? Do you know what you need to learn so that you get the full benefit of your strengths? Few have even asked themselves these questions."**

Do you know what's exciting? There's this excellent tool that was whipped up by the brilliant minds at the Gallup Foundation. It's a game-changer, and it's not only for the sake of saying.

The tool is named as the Strengths Finder 2.0 Test and can be done online. The test report will help you know your areas of maximum power and areas of most significant limitations. The report will also provide you with very precise advice on how to play to your strengths in day-to-day life and deal with your weaknesses.

**When you align your life to your key strengths, you will enter the magical zone of Ease, Enjoyment and Excellence!!!**

I took the Strengths Finder 2.0 Test many years ago, and wow, it's made such a difference for me. It's been a game-changer in my life, and the people I coach have seen incredible results too!

Now, after finding your strengths, the next step is pretty thrilling. It's about picturing your life 5 years from now & asking yourself the question:

**What does a beautiful life look like for me?**

And when you're mulling over that, think about all the roles you play in your life.

Let this question stew in your mind a bit. As you give it ample time and attention, the correct answers **shall appear.**

Remember, creating a beautiful life isn't a sprint; it's more of a marathon. So take your time, reflect, and let the magic happen!

The true secret to a beautiful life isn't in reaching the destination, but in embracing the journey itself. It's about living a life on a day-to-day basis that resonates with your soul, one that's beautifully yours.

You're the architect of your own life, capable of designing and cherishing your masterpiece. Remember, it's your DUTY to shape it. **If not you, then who?**

Chapter 3

# Threads of Grace: Exploring the Dynamic Duo of Help and Gratitude

## Unveiling Help: Universe's Boundless Key

It was only when I delved into the dictionary definition of 'help,' which was defined as: **to make it easier or possible for someone to do something,** I truly understood its profound essence. As I began to view the world through the prism of help, its presence became apparent everywhere.

This realization didn't occur instantaneously. It emerged gradually like the rising sun dispersing the morning fog. Within every interaction, relationship, and decision, a subtle dance of help unfolded. I began to perceive many dimensions of help.

The epiphany dawned on me: Help is one of the Universe's greatest secrets!

**The great philosopher, L. Ron Hubbard, has beautifully said "The reason life is life and people are together, and the grass grows, and trees grow and apparently the rain falls and everything else, is because it helps somebody."**

This book I'm writing, also serves as a testament to the power of help. It couldn't have come into being without the contribution of so many people who have made it possible.

## When Help Prevailed

As I reflect on the incredible power of help, my mind drifts back to heart-wrenching events that unfolded during the peak of the Delta variant surge in Delhi. It was a period when the community faced unprecedented challenges, yet it was also a time when the true spirit of collective assistance radiated brilliantly.

In every corner of the city, individuals took personal responsibility for their safety, understanding that by helping themselves, they were protecting others too. This heightened sense of self-care seamlessly transitioned into a profound desire to help others. Neighbours transformed into pillars of support, extending a helping hand in any way possible, ensuring that no one faced the battle alone.

However, it didn't stop there. Individuals from various backgrounds emerged as volunteers, dedicating their time and expertise to assist overwhelmed healthcare facilities. The spirit of help spread like ripples, turning strangers into allies, who collaborated to set up community kitchens and provide nourishment for the vulnerable.

The response was automatic, an unwritten agreement among the people of Delhi to come together and extend help to one another. The community worked harmoniously, converting schools and community centres into improvised hospitals, arranging transportation for medical emergencies, and setting up helplines to connect individuals with essential resources.

Amidst the darkest days, their unwavering resilience became a beacon of hope for the rest of the world. They faced the challenges head-on, adapting and innovating to meet the needs of the hour. The collective help witnessed in Delhi during the Delta variant outbreak showcased the power of unity, solidarity, and compassion.

This heart-wrenching tale is a testament to the extraordinary impact of individuals coming together in the face of adversity. It serves as a reminder that our collective strength knows no bounds when we stand united, reaching out to those in need. The people of Delhi epitomized the true essence of humanity, demonstrating that even amidst one of the most significant crises humanity has ever encountered, the natural human instinct to help prevails.

## The Interdependence Effect

When I look back on my journey, I noticed the numerous individuals who have played a crucial role in shaping my life—parents, family members, relatives, teachers, philosophers, mentors, friends, role models, coaches and many more. Each person has made a distinct and invaluable contribution, leaving a lasting impact on my character and destiny.

Seeking help wasn't a sign of weakness but an acknowledgement of interdependence, serving as a testament to our shared humanity.

This realization brought not only liberation but also deepened my connections with others. The more I sought help, the more friendships I forged, and my understanding of both myself and others expanded in the process.

By acknowledging our interdependence and recognizing the role of help in our survival, we gain a clearer perspective of our strengths and weaknesses.

We can seek help from those who possess strengths in areas we may lack, fostering tremendous growth and progress.

Please note that help isn't always about grand gestures. Whether it's a shared idea, a word of encouragement, or even a smile, help takes many forms, and each one is valuable. The most significant impacts are often made in minor acts.

## The Gratitude Connection

Gratitude is more than just saying "thank you." It involves truly appreciating the help we've received and recognizing the individuals who've contributed to making our journey more manageable, prosperous, and meaningful. It's an attitude, a way of life that centers on acknowledging the positive aspects even in the face of adversity..

Gratitude is a positive emotion that directs our attention to the good aspects of our lives. It involves taking a moment to notice and appreciate the things we often take for granted—such as our home, food, clean water, friends, family, and even our access to technology.

**As Oprah Winfrey wisely said, "Be thankful for what you have; you'll end up having more. If you concentrate on what you don't have, you will never, ever have enough."**

The beauty of gratitude lies in its ability to remind us of our blessings, shifting our focus on abundance rather than scarcity. As we cultivate an attitude of gratitude, we naturally attract more positivity and goodness into our lives.

**Alfred North White head has said, "No one who achieves success does so without the help of others. The wise and confident acknowledge this help with gratitude."**

As I realized the contribution of many people in shaping my life, a profound sense of gratitude emerged within me. I created a list of all those who had helped me, acknowledging the ways they had done so. This simple act revealed the tremendous power I was surrounded by and the wealth of blessings I had received, transforming me into a much more certain, calmer, more empathetic and wiser individual.

My coachees who embrace gratitude cultivate resilience, strengthen relationships, and enhance performance in all aspects of life. With a mindset of abundance and possibility, they are able to achieve seemingly impossible goals and live wholeheartedly.

I hope this chapter has widened your perspective on the concept of help and guided you towards a deeper understanding of gratitude. As you continue your journey, remember to take moments to pause, observe, and appreciate the everyday miracles around you.

In conclusion, let's engage in an exercise of self-reflection and gratitude. Make a list of all the individuals who have helped you in your life's journey; against each name, note down all the things you are grateful to that person for. As you do this, you will cultivate a heightened awareness and appreciation for the Universe's grace that often goes unnoticed.

# Building High Trust Relationships: A Path to Joy and Fulfilment

**When you hear the term "relationship," who appears in your mind?**

Is it your spouse, parents, children, or maybe your friends? But how often do you think about your relationship with yourself or your team members?

Relationships come in all shapes and sizes - personal, professional, and, most importantly, the one you have with yourself. Each relationship is like a unique jigsaw puzzle piece, adding value and meaning to our lives.

A revelation that may astonish you is this: the foundation of all relationships, irrespective of their nature, is trust.

**What is Trust?**

The dictionary definition of trust is: to believe that someone or something is reliable, good, honest, effective, etc. or to have confidence in (someone or something).

Another definition is: feeling safe when vulnerable.

When we depend on a leader, family member or friend, we can feel vulnerable, and we need trust to manage the anxiety of this feeling. When trust is present, things go well; but when trust is lost, the relationship is at risk.

As Romanoff puts it, **"Trust is the foundation of every relationship; it allows us to lower our guard, be vulnerable, and truly connect."**

High-trust relationships within a professional environment offer incredible advantages.

Envision a workspace where collaboration is the standard, innovative thoughts flow freely, and productivity reaches new heights. It may seem like an idealistic vision. But that's the power of high trust! When employees feel more engaged and satisfied, it nurtures a sense of loyalty towards the organization, creating a mutually beneficial situation!

The beauty of high-trust relationships extends far beyond the boundaries of your workspace. It permeates our personal lives, nurturing open communication, fostering deep emotional connections, promoting mutual growth, and shared responsibilities. Such is the transformative power of trust in intimate relationships.

However, the journey towards high-trust relationships can be challenging. It's a rugged terrain scattered with stumbling blocks.

**Remember the insightful words of Stephen Covey? "We judge ourselves by our intentions and others by their actions."**

This inherent bias in judgment can lead to ineffective communication, causing rifts in our relationships.

**So, how do we cultivate high-trust relationships?**

To start, assessing yourself on your actions and others based on their intentions.

Next, consider trust as a bank account with deposits and withdrawals.

To enhance trust, strive to minimize withdrawals and consistently make deposits.

**Dissecting Withdrawals**

1. **Gossiping:** Speaking negatively about others, especially behind their backs, indicates that you might do the same to the people you're conversing with. This can create hesitation in them to share personal information or participate in meaningful conversations.

2. **Ignoring or Dismissing Feelings:** Neglecting or disregarding the emotions or perspectives of others can make them feel invalidated. This can lead to them being less open and less likely to seek your support or advice.

3. **Being Defensive:** Reacting negatively or defensively to feedback can create an unwelcoming environment. People might hesitate to share their views and be less receptive to your feedback.

4. **Avoiding Responsibility:** Shifting blame or not accepting your mistakes suggests a lack of accountability, which can raise doubts about your integrity and reliability, making people hesitant to depend on you.

5. **Inconsistency Between Words and Actions:** When your actions don't align with your words, it breeds confusion and uncertainty, causing people to doubt your reliability, making them cautious about trusting your promises.

6. **Violating Boundaries:** Repeatedly crossing personal or professional boundaries indicates a lack of respect for the other person's comfort and autonomy. It can make people uncomfortable, prompting them to distance themselves.

To preserve strong relationships, it's crucial to consistently demonstrate respect, honesty, accountability, and integrity, remaining mindful of how your actions can impact others.

## Dissecting Deposits

1. **Actively Listen:** Active listening involves understanding the underlying message, showing interest, and responding thoughtfully. It shows others that they are important for you.

2. **Be Honest:** Honesty isn't limited to not lying; it also involves being transparent about your thoughts and feelings. Authenticity, even in challenging situations, is highly valued.

3. **Show Respect:** Acknowledge others' ideas, provide them space, and treat them kindly. Respectful disagreements play a crucial role in fostering healthy relationships.

4. **Admit Mistakes:** Own your mistakes, apologize sincerely, and rectify them. It displays humility and willingness to learn, fostering respect and understanding.

5. **Be Reliable:** Consistency in following through with your commitments reassures people they can rely on you.

6. **Provide Support:** Being available in times of need and offering help and comfort reassures others that they can rely on you during tough times.

7. **Show Appreciation:** Express gratitude when others help you or do a good job. It makes others feel valued and respected.

8. **Consistency:** Maintain predictability in your actions. When people can anticipate your responses based on past experiences, they're more likely to feel comfortable and at ease with you.

Remember, high-trust relationships are built or destroyed by one conversation or one act at a time.

You can nurture positive, strong, and enduring relationships by fostering these behaviours consistently.

As we conclude this chapter, I urge you to reflect on this question:

**How can I infuse more trust and joy into my relationships?**

Cultivating high-trust relationships may be arduous, but the rewards are certainly worth it. It's akin to nurturing a seed, observing it sprout and bloom into a gorgeous plant. Let's nourish the seeds of trust in our relationships and collaborate to create a flourishing garden of joy, fulfilment, and mutual growth.

# Conclusion

As we approach the end of this book, "Get 10X Done," I am deeply grateful for the opportunity to share these transformative principles with you.

I sincerely hope that the insights shared within these pages have sparked a new perspective and ignited a fresh motivation within you. Your decision to delve into this book demonstrates your remarkable commitment to personal growth, and I commend you for this.

As you continue on your journey, remember that each step is a part of a greater narrative. Your story is both unique and beautiful, defined by your experiences, triumphs, and even setbacks. Each one is a thread in the fabric of your life, weaving together to create a pattern of growth, resilience, and success.

Serving as your guide has been an honour, and your trust humbles me.

Remember, this journey does not end here; it is only the beginning. As you step forward, you are entering a future teeming with endless possibilities as you embrace the power of duty, the strength of vision, the joy of gratitude, and the warmth of high-trust relationships. These qualities will guide you and accompany you on your path to success and fulfillment.

Here's to your journey to 10X success. I wish you courage, joy, and fulfilment in all your endeavours. Keep aspiring, keep growing, and remember – you can accomplish extraordinary things!

Much Love,

Rajiv Pasricha

# Connect with Me

Dear Reader,

I would be delighted to hear about your experiences and the transformations you have experienced due to the principles shared in this book. Your feedback is invaluable and will contribute significantly to my ongoing work and future publications.

You can connect with me directly at **book1@get10xdone.in** Whether you share your journey, ask questions, or provide feedback, I look forward to hearing from you.

Remember, this is not the end but merely the beginning of a remarkable journey. Let's continue on this path together towards achieving 10X success!

Warm Regards,

Rajiv Pasricha

Business & Leadership Coach

www.get10xdone.in

## NOTES:

## NOTES:

## NOTES: